DINOSAUR ZOOM!

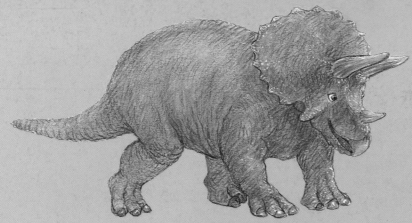

Triceratops

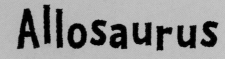
Allosaurus

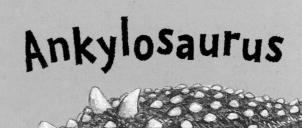
Ankylosaurus

Iguanodon

Carnotaurus

Megalosaurus

Stegosaurus

Baryonyx

Styracosaurus

Tyrannosaurus
rex

For Bryan

First published 2012 by Nosy Crow Ltd
The Crow's Nest, 10a Lant Street
London SE1 1QR
www.nosycrow.com

ISBN 978 0 85763 080 3 (HB)
ISBN 978 0 85763 081 0 (PB)

Nosy Crow and associated logos are trademark
and or registered trademarks of Nosy Crow Ltd.

A CIP catalogue record for this book is available from the British Library.

Printed in China

1 3 5 7 9 8 6 4 2

DINOSAUR ZOOM!

Penny Dale

nosy crow

Red dinosaur driving,
driving through the desert.
Through the desert, dust and sand.

zoom!

Zoom!

Zooooom!

Brown dinosaur racing,
racing through the rain.

Through the rain,
and round the bend.

Splash!

Splash!

Blue dinosaur climbing,
climbing up the mountain.

Up the mountain,
past rocks and snow.

Brrmm!

Brrmmm!

Brrmmm!

Green dinosaur rattling, rattling down the hill.

Down the hill, with a heavy load.

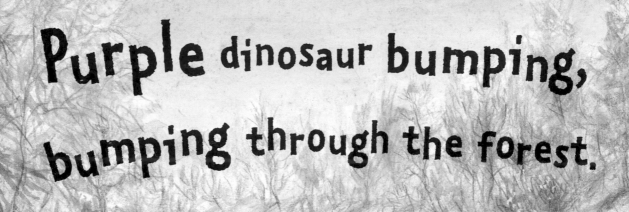

Purple dinosaur bumping, bumping through the forest.

Through the forest, along rocky tracks.

Rrrrmm!

Rrrrmm!

Orange dinosaur jumping, jumping over puddles.

Over puddles, skidding and squelching.

Bounce! Bounce!

Bounce!

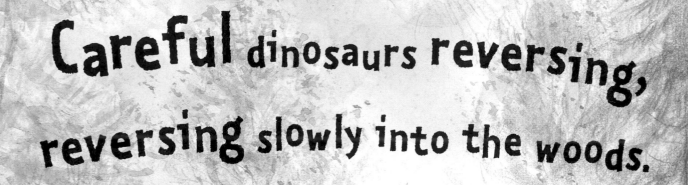

Careful dinosaurs reversing,
reversing slowly into the woods.

Into the woods,
with a special load.

Beep!

Beep!

Beep!

Busy dinosaurs hurrying,
hurrying to get ready.

To get everything ready in time.

Excited dinosaurs hiding,
hiding and trying not to move.

Getting ready...
getting ready for a BIG...

A surprise
party!

A party for...

the littlest dinosaur!

A party with **presents!**

...and a GREAT BIG cake!

Convertible

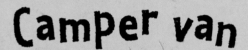

Camper van

Off-road vehicle

Tractor and trailer

Motorbike

Pick-up
truck

Breakdown
truck

Electric
sports car